MW01714329

HORROR- The Diaries Of Darkness

Mortaza Tokhy

Published by True American Publishing, 2023.

This is a work of fiction. Similarities to real people, places, or events are entirely coincidental.

HORROR- THE DIARIES OF DARKNESS

First edition. July 10, 2023.

ISBN: 979-8223500964

Written by Mortaza Tokhy.

The Lacking City

Prologue

IT WAS DUSK ON A WARM, summer day when I first saw a dead body. Mitch and I rode our bikes down the dirt road to the old town known as The Lacking City. Uncertainty and fear churned in my gut like bubbling oil. We had heard stories about the bodies that were said to haunt the ruined buildings, but now we were less than two blocks from the town hall and I could not turn back. It was as if a magnetic field was pulling us forward into its mysterious heart. My legs propelled me down the street, along with Mitch's, who followed closely behind. We stopped just outside of town limits on a gravel lot where we parked our bikes next to an abandoned blue van. A sense of dread shot through me and I felt frozen to my seat. Then I noticed it: a faint light flickering off in the distance near one of the many crumbling houses. As if drawn by a flame, we both moved towards it at once.

CHAPTER 1

Through the jagged hole in the window, I could see a candle flickering on a table. The light curved around the uneven walls of the room and flickered like fireflies in summer air. As we got closer, we heard a soft whisper, like someone was singing a song. The hairs on the back of my neck stood on end, and I could feel my heart pounding in my chest. We crept up to the door, and I pushed it open with a careless shove. The whispering grew louder as we climbed the stairs, and when we reached the top, we saw what caused the noise.

THERE, IN THE MIDDLE of the room, lay a girl. Her body was young and thin, hardly more than a child's. She was dressed in a silky white gown that flowed around her like a veil of fog. Her eyes were closed, and she held a small, black book in her hands. As we approached, she lifted her head and looked at us with a blank stare.

THEN, WITH A SUDDEN jolt, she sprang to her feet and began to speak in a language I had never heard before. Her words were a flurry of syllables that sounded like they were from another world. Mitch and I stood frozen, not knowing what to do or say. The girl's eyes shone with an unearthly light, and she fell back down onto the floor, her body shaking with convulsions.

I RAN TO HER SIDE, trying to catch her flailing arms. "What's wrong?" I yelled. My voice was lost in the chanting around us. She thrashed at me and then collapsed into my arms like a rag doll. Her eyes were wide open and unseeing. A terrible thought jumped to mind: Was she blind? Had years of magic been inflicted on her? But the girl didn't respond. Instead, she began to vomit a thick, black substance that reeked of sulfur. The smell was suffocating, and it made my eyes water and my stomach churn. A sense of panic began to overtake me, and I knew we had to get out of there - fast. Mitch grabbed my arm and pulled me towards the door. "Come on, we have to go!"

WE STUMBLED DOWN THE stairs and out the door, gasping for air. The smell of sulfur still lingered in my nostrils, and I felt like I was going to be sick. As we stepped out into the night, we saw that the once-flickering candles had now gone out and darkness had consumed the old mansion. We mounted our bikes and rode away from The Lacking City as fast as we could, our hearts pounding in our chests.

WHEN WE WERE FINALLY out of sight of the old town, we stopped to catch our breath. "What the hell was that?" I asked, still shaking with fear.

"I DON'T KNOW," MITCH replied, his face pale. "But I think we should go to the police." We'd both realized that going to the police meant admitting that we had snuck into The Lacking City, but we also knew what we had seen was too dangerous to ignore. We knew that the world needed heroes, and so we put our pride aside and hurried over to the police station. The uniformed officer looked at us with a mixture of suspicion and confusion, but we didn't care. We had found people who could help.

AS WE LEFT THE POLICE station, I knew that the officer didn't believe our story. This meant that Mitch and I would have to investigate this ourselves.

CHAPTER 2

Anxiously, we returned to The Lacking City, determined to find out what had happened to the girl. We started our search at the old mansion, where it all made sense. We brought flashlights, ropes, and our cellphones fully charged. Once inside the mansion, we made our way up the stairs to the room where we had found the girl. The room was empty compared with how it looked a few days ago. Less furniture filled it and most of the books were gone from the shelves. Still nothing seemed out of place except for one small detail: on a table by the window sat an old pair of binoculars.

JUST AS WE WERE ABOUT to give up, we noticed a small door hidden behind a bookcase. We pulled the bookcase aside to reveal a narrow staircase leading down into darkness. Without hesitation, we descended the stairs and found ourselves in a small, dimly lit room. It was a makeshift laboratory, filled with dusty jars and bottles, strange tools, and even stranger books. As we looked around in awe, we heard a faint whispering sound. We followed the sound to the back of the room, where we found a small table covered in an array of odd herbs and powders. On the table lay a book, its pages filled with strange symbols and diagrams.

"THIS MUST BE THE BOOK the girl was holding," I whispered to Mitch. He nodded and reached out to pick it up, but as his hand touched the cover, the room began to shake. The jars and bottles on the shelves rattled and clinked, and the ground beneath our feet trembled. "We have to get out of here!" I yelled, grabbing Mitch's arm and pulling him towards the staircase.

WE RAN UP THE STAIRS as fast as we could, but just as we reached the top, the door slammed shut behind us. We were trapped.

Suddenly, the chanting began again, louder and more intense than before. The walls of the room vibrated with the force of it, the cacophony becoming a mallet pounding against my brain. Mitch and I huddled together, too scared to even speak. I could see a faded image at the far end of the room.

IT WAS A FIGURE, CLOAKED in black and standing in front of a large, ornate mirror. It was chanting in a language even more foreign than the girl from the night before. I could see its breath fogging up the mirror as it continued to chant, the sound growing louder and more intense with each passing moment.

Suddenly, the mirror began to glow, casting an eerie light throughout the room. The figure in black stepped back, and I saw its reflection in the mirror - it was not human. Its eyes were black and soulless, and its skin was a sickly gray color. It continued to chant in its foreign tongue, and I could feel the ground beneath us trembling harder and harder.

AS THE FIGURE RAISED its arms, I knew we were in grave danger. Mitch and I huddled together, unsure of what to do next. Just as the figure was about to make its move, there was a loud explosion, and the room was plunged into darkness. We heard the sound of footsteps running towards us, and then a voice called out, "Are you guys, okay?"

IT WAS THE POLICE OFFICER from the previous night. He had followed us to The Lacking City and had heard the explosion. He had found the hidden door and had managed to shut off the power source that was fueling the strange rituals.

WE STUMBLED OUT OF the mansion, still in shock, and were immediately taken to the police station. We recounted everything we had seen and heard to the officer, who listened intently. When we finished, he told us that he had already called in a team of experts to investigate the mansion and the strange occurrences that had taken place there.

DAYS LATER, WE RECEIVED a call from the officer. He told us that the team had discovered an underground network of tunnels beneath The Lacking City, which had been used by a secret society to perform dark rituals and experiments. The girl we had seen was likely a victim of their experiments, and the book we had found was a key component of their rituals.

THE SOCIETY HAD BEEN operating in secret for years, and the police had never suspected a thing. But thanks to our investigation, they were finally able to put a stop to their nefarious activities.

Mitch and I were hailed as heroes for our bravery, but we both knew that we had just scratched the surface of the dark secrets hidden beneath The Lacking City.

CHAPTER 3

Over the following weeks, we pored over the notes and materials we had gathered from the mansion, trying to piece together the true nature of the society and its goals. We discovered that they had been experimenting with dark magic and other-worldly beings, seeking to gain power and knowledge beyond human comprehension.

DESPITE THE DANGER, we were both inexplicably drawn to the mysteries of The Lacking City, and we continued to explore its secrets even as the police closed in on the remaining members of the society.

AS WE DELVED DEEPER into the dark, the air became heavy and damp. It was as if we were sinking into a grave, walls of stone growing up around us. Our torch illuminated only a foot or so in front of us, leaving the rest of our path in darkness. We could hear water dripping from above, drops pattering against the floor and echoing off the walls. The officer told us that we were chasing after something inhuman. A primal fear grew in me then, an urge to return what I had already found and run back to my machines and their safety.

THE MORE WE UNCOVERED, the more we realized that the society had opened a portal to another dimension, one filled with unspeakable horrors that were now seeping into our world. We knew that we had to stop them before it was too late, but we also knew that we were in over our heads.

WE SOUGHT OUT EXPERTS in the field of the occult, hoping to find someone who could help us understand what we were dealing with.

We found a woman named Dr. Isabella Blackwood, a renowned scholar of the paranormal. She listened to our story with a grave expression and then agreed to help us.

TOGETHER, WE BEGAN to study the notes and materials we had gathered, trying to decipher the strange symbols and diagrams that filled the pages of the book we had found. Dr. Blackwood explained that the symbols were part of a complex system of magic, one that had been used by ancient civilizations to harness the power of other dimensions. As we delved deeper into the research, we began to experience strange phenomena ourselves. We would hear whispers in the night, feel cold chills run down our spines, and see shadowy figures lurking in the corners of our vision. We knew that the society we had uncovered had somehow opened a portal to another dimension, and that they had unleashed unspeakable horrors into our world.

CHAPTER 4

Dr. Blackwood warned us that we were playing with forces beyond our comprehension, and that the only way to stop the society was to close the portal. But to do that, we would need to find a way to harness the power of the same magic they had been using.

WE SPENT MONTHS STUDYING the ancient texts and experimenting with different spells and rituals. We worked tirelessly, driven by a sense of urgency and a deep-seated fear of what would happen if we failed.

FINALLY, AFTER WHAT seemed like an eternity, we found the key to closing the portal. We gathered our materials, made our way to The Lacking City, and began to perform the ritual.

THE AIR AROUND US GREW thick with energy, and we could feel the power of the magic coursing through our bodies. We chanted in unison, calling forth the ancient forces that lay beyond the portal. The ground shook beneath our feet, and the sky above us turned dark and foreboding.

AS WE WORKED, WE COULD hear the screams of the society members as they fought against us, trying to protect their dark secrets and keep the portal open. But we were determined and focused, and we chanted louder and more intensely with each passing moment.

AND THEN, JUST AS WE felt our strength beginning to wane, we heard a loud crackling sound. A bright light filled the sky, and the ground trembled beneath us. We knew that we had succeeded - the portal was closing.

The deep blue sky we had seen only moments before was beginning to fade into a pastel haze. Slowly, the ground beneath us stopped shaking. We looked around, relieved and exhausted, and saw that the society members had all disappeared. After I caught my breath I knew one thing for sure: it wasn't over yet.

DAYS AFTER WE CLOSED the portal, strange things began to happen in The Lacking City. People reported seeing shadowy figures lurking in the alleys, and the air was thick with an ominous energy. It was as though the society's experiments had taken on a life of their own, and were now roaming freely throughout the city.

Mitch and I knew that we had to act fast. We contacted Dr. Blackwood, who agreed to help us once again. Together, we devised a plan to try and contain the creatures before they could do any more damage.

CHAPTER 5

We gathered our materials and set out into the city, searching for any sign of the otherworldly beings. We encountered a few at first, but with the help of our magic and Dr. Blackwood's knowledge, we were able to contain them.

BUT AS WE WENT DEEPER into the city, we realized that there were more of them than we could have ever imagined. They were everywhere - crawling out of the shadows and slinking through

THE STREETS LIKE FERAL beasts. We fought them one by one, using every ounce of our strength to contain them. It was a grueling battle, but we refused to give up. We knew that if we failed, the creatures would continue to wreak havoc on The Lacking City, and innocent people would suffer. We fought until we were exhausted, and then we fought some more.

FINALLY, AFTER WHAT felt like an eternity, we managed to contain most of the creatures. We stood in the middle of the empty street, panting and covered in sweat, and looked around at the devastation. Mitch and I knew it wasn't over.

WE KNEW THAT THERE were still more creatures lurking in the darkness, waiting to pounce on unsuspecting victims. We knew that we had only contained them temporarily, and that they would eventually break free again. But we refused to give up. We had come too far and sacrificed too much to let the creatures win. We vowed to continue fighting until we had rid The Lacking City of their presence once and for all.

CHAPTER 6

We spent the next few weeks researching and preparing for the next battle. We reached out to other experts in the field of the paranormal, gathering as much information and support as we could. We studied the creatures' weaknesses and developed new spells and rituals to fight them.

AND THEN, ONE NIGHT, we set out into the city once again. We moved quietly, our eyes scanning the shadows for any sign of movement. We knew that the creatures were out there, waiting for us. Suddenly, a rustling sound came from behind us. We spun around, ready for battle, but to our surprise, we saw a figure emerging from the darkness. It was a woman, dressed in tattered clothes and covered in dirt and grime. She looked at us with wild, frightened eyes, and we could tell that she had been living on the streets for a long time.

AT FIRST, WE WERE WARY of her. We had seen what the creatures were capable of, and we couldn't risk letting our guard down. But as she approached us, we saw that she was trembling with fear and desperation.

"MY NAME IS SARAH," she said, her voice shaking. "Please, I need your help. I've been hiding from those things for weeks, and I don't know how much longer I can survive."

Our hearts went out to her, and we knew that we couldn't turn her away. We explained to her the danger that she was in, and she agreed to help us in any way that she could.

TOGETHER, THE THREE of us tried to find the entrance to the city. It was gone. We searched in desperation but it was gone. We knew we were, just like the woman stuck in The Lacking City with no way out.

AS THE REALITY OF OUR situation sank in, we realized that we were not just fighting against the creatures, but against the very fabric of the city itself. The Lacking City had become a prison, trapping us inside with no way out.

CHAPTER 7

We tried everything we could think of to escape, but each attempt was met with failure. The city seemed to be actively working against us - walls shifted and moved, paths we had taken before suddenly led to dead ends, and even our magic seemed to be less effective within its boundaries.

DAYS TURNED INTO WEEKS, and weeks turned into months. We fought the creatures whenever they appeared, but our spirits were starting to falter. We were tired, hungry, and beginning to lose hope.

BUT THEN, SOMETHING strange started to happen. The creatures began to avoid us, as if they were afraid of something. We couldn't explain it - they had always been relentless in their pursuit of us before. But now, they seemed to be actively avoiding us.

IT WASN'T UNTIL ONE night, when we stumbled upon a strange glow in the distance, that we realized what was happening. We cautiously approached, and as we got closer, we saw that the glow was emanating from a massive portal in the middle of the city.

WE KNEW THAT THIS PORTAL was different from the one we had closed before - it was much more powerful, more unstable. But we also knew that it was our only chance at escaping The Lacking City.

WITH RENEWED DETERMINATION, we began to make our way towards the portal, fighting off any creatures that dared to stand in our way. As we got closer, the ground beneath our feet began to shake, and the air grew thick with energy.

WE COULD FEEL THE POWER of the portal coursing through our bodies, and we knew that we had to act quickly before it consumed us completely. We chanted in unison, using all of our magic to keep the portal stable as we stepped through.

THE LIGHT WAS BLINDING, and we felt ourselves being pulled through a vortex of swirling colors and shapes. We could hear the wailing of the creatures behind us as they were consumed by the portal's power.

FINALLY, WE EMERGED on the other side - gasping for air and covered in sweat and dirt. We looked around, disoriented and unsure of where we were. But as our eyes adjusted to the new environment, we realized that we had made it out.

WE WERE FREE. WE COLLAPSED on the ground, tears streaming down our faces and aching backs. We were exhausted. The creatures were gone, defeated by the last of our weapons. We had escaped The Lacking City. It was then we realized that the woman we had discovered on the streets in the city wasn't with us. I looked at Mitch and we both knew we would have to find a way back into The Lacking City to save her. "No way "cried Mitch "I'm not ever going in there again"

BUT I KNEW WE COULDN'T leave Sarah behind. She had risked everything to help us, and we couldn't abandon her now. I looked at Mitch determinedly, "We have to try, Mitch. She's out there, alone and scared. We can't just leave her behind."

Mitch looked at me for a long moment, his expression conflicted. But then he nodded slowly, "Okay. But we have to be careful. We don't know what we're up against."

WE SPENT THE NEXT FEW days preparing ourselves for the journey back into The Lacking City. We gathered our weapons, stocked up on supplies, and studied as much as we could about the city's layout and the creatures that inhabited it.

AND THEN ONE NIGHT, we walked back into the city. It was different than we remembered. It was quiet and as normal as a regular city. The air glowed with soft amber lights that cast everything in a decadent, honeyed glow. There were people going about their business. Something was wrong. Were we in The Lacking City or was this a parallel city?

WE CAUTIOUSLY WALKED down the empty streets, our eyes scanning every corner for any sign of danger. The buildings loomed over us, casting long shadows in the amber light. It felt familiar, yet different at the same time.

AS WE TURNED A CORNER, we saw her - Sarah. She was sitting on the pavement, her back against a wall, her eyes closed. We rushed over to her, worried that she might be hurt. “Sarah, can you hear me?” I asked anxiously, kneeling beside her. Her eyes flickered open, and she glanced at me, confusion in her gaze. “Who are you?” she murmured softly. Her words pierced my heart; not only did she not recognize us, but also the fact that her memory had vanished from her mind was agonizing for Mitch and me.

WE EXCHANGED A WORRIED glance, unsure of what to do next. But then, we noticed something strange - there was a glowing symbol etched onto her forehead. It was unlike anything we had ever seen before, and we knew that it held some kind of power.

WITHOUT HESITATION, we began to chant a spell. The air around us grew thick with magic, and the symbol on Sarah's forehead began to pulse with a bright light.

AND THEN, IN AN INSTANT, her memory returned. She gasped, clutching her head in pain as the memories flooded back to her. "What happened?" she cried out, looking at us with wide eyes. "I can't leave this place, I'm not what you think I am, I'm not human like you" I come from a different world, a world of magic and mystery. I was sent here to find a way to close the portal that had opened between our worlds. But something went wrong - I got trapped here, and my memory was wiped clean."

WE LISTENED TO HER story, our eyes widening with each passing moment. We couldn't believe what we were hearing - that Sarah was from another world, and that she had been sent here with a mission. But what about the other people in the city. They seemed so normal.

SARAH EXPLAINED THAT the people in the city were not real. They were simply an illusion created by the city's magic, designed to make it seem like a normal place. In reality, the city was a gateway between worlds, and it was up to us to close the portal before it destroyed everything.

WE KNEW THAT IT WOULDN'T be easy, but we were determined to see it through to the end. With Sarah's help, we began to explore the city once again, searching for any clues that would lead us to the portal.

THIS TIME, WE HAD COME prepared; our sacks were filled with food that we anticipated would be a necessity. We marched with determination, the weight of sustenance dragging us down, knowing that this was our only chance to survive. Our future rested upon it.

MY HEART SKIPPED A beat as I spun around to find Sarah vanished without a trace. Mitch's face grew pale, and he screamed, "This is why I said we shouldn't come back! We're in deep trouble now!" His words were laden with fear and dread as his eyes searched hopelessly for any sign of her. "We have to move on Mitch. We can't stay here," I said with some hesitation.

I TURNED MY FACE AWAY from Mitch and couldn't look him in the eyes. "We have to move on Mitch. We can't stay here," I said with some hesitation. The stillness between us seemed to stretch forth into eternity.

CHAPTER 8

I was certain Sarah wasn't with us. It almost seemed like she was a product of our collective imagination. But then, a glimmer caught my eye, drawing my attention to a dark alleyway. I motioned for Mitch to follow me as we cautiously approached the source of the light.

AS WE GOT CLOSER, WE saw that it was Sarah - her body was glowing with a soft, blue light. She was chanting a spell, her voice low and melodic. We watched in awe as the magic began to swirl around her, coalescing into a bright, shining ball of light.

AND THEN, WITH A FINAL burst of energy, the ball of light shot out of her hands and into the sky, creating a massive explosion of color and sound. The air around us crackled with magic as the portal began to close, its power dissipating into nothingness.

We exchanged a look of relief and gratitude towards Sarah, realizing that without her help, we would have never been able to escape The Lacking City.

AS WE MADE OUR WAY out of the city, I turned and looked behind me. The softball-sized fireball moved through the streets quickly, sending fiery debris in every direction. The crowd of people who were once there before now disintegrated into dust and bone. I heard screams coming from Sarah. The Lacking City no longer existed. Gone was the cloud of dust that covered the city's edges; gone was the wall of hardened black glass; gone were the houses and buildings that once stood tall.

THE NEXT MORNING AS I awoke I could hear my mother cooking breakfast. I quickly got dressed and went downstairs. My mother was standing at the stove, flipping pancakes with a smile on her face. It was as if nothing had happened, as if The Lacking City and Sarah's world had never existed.

I SAT DOWN AT THE TABLE, feeling numb and disoriented. Had it all been a dream? But then, I saw the symbol on my hand - it was the same symbol that had been on Sarah's forehead. It was a reminder that our adventure was real, that we had saved a world and escaped a dangerous city.

BUT AS I LOOKED AROUND the kitchen, I couldn't help but wonder how many other worlds were out there, waiting to be discovered. And I knew that one day, I would venture forth again, ready to face whatever dangers lay ahead.

THE HIDDEN CHAMBER

Josh was excited for his first day at summer camp. He had never been away from home before and was slightly nervous. He had packed his bags the night before, and now he was standing in line with all the other kids, waiting to be assigned to cabins. He looked around, taking in all the new faces and new surroundings. He was a little intimidated, but he was also eager to explore.

WHEN JOSH WAS FINALLY assigned to a cabin, he found himself bunking with two other boys his age, both of whom seemed just as eager to explore their new home. The three of them quickly became friends, and for the first few days, they spent their time running around the camp, playing sports, and exploring the woods nearby.

ONE DAY, WHILE THE three were playing in the woods, they found a hidden cave. Josh was the first to step inside, and when he did, he was filled with a sense of wonder. The cave walls were lined with ancient carvings, and strange symbols were etched into the ground.

THEY SOON FOUND AN old, rusty key partially hidden in the dust as they kept exploring. Josh picked it up and held it in his hand. He could feel a strange energy radiating, and he knew this must be a unique find.

WHEN HE HELD THE KEY up to the light, he noticed it had strange markings, like writing, etched onto its surface. He couldn't determine what it said, but he knew this was no ordinary key. He could feel the power that it held.

HE SHOWED HIS NEW FRIENDS the key and told them about the strange feeling he was getting from it. They were both intrigued as well, although a bit skeptical. But Josh could tell that they were both excited to explore the possibilities of this mysterious object.

THE NEXT DAY, THE THREE of them explored the cave further. Josh held the key in his hand, guiding them through the darkness. As they walked, they noticed strange things happening around them. Doors started to appear in the walls where they hadn't been before, and when they opened them, they revealed hidden chambers filled with mysterious objects and strange treasures.

THEY KEPT EXPLORING for what felt like hours until they finally came to the end of the cave. They found a large iron door with a strange, intricate lock. Josh held up the key, and to their amazement, it fit perfectly into the lock.

WHEN HE TURNED THE key, the door slowly opened, revealing a hidden chamber beyond. They found a beautiful crystal chamber filled with mysterious artifacts and strange symbols inside. They were all filled with awe and wonder as they explored the chamber and its strange objects.

JOSH LOOKED AROUND in amazement. He knew this key must have magical powers and couldn't wait to explore it further. He thanked his friends for coming and explored the magical treasures without them.

As Josh placed the key in one of the doors, the walls around him began to move closer together.

HIS HEART RACED AS he realized he was trapped, but he knew he had to remain calm. Josh tried to find his way back to where his friends were, but the walls continued to shift, and he soon found himself in a small, dark chamber with no doors or windows.

JOSH COULD FEEL HIS breathing quickening as he panicked, wondering how to get out. But then he remembered the key. He held it up to the dim light in the room and noticed it glowing softly, radiating warm, comforting energy. Taking a deep breath, he closed his eyes and concentrated on the key. Suddenly, he felt a jolt of energy coursing through his body. He opened his eyes, and to his amazement, he could see the walls around him beginning to shift and change.

AS HE WATCHED IN AWE, the walls began to morph and twist, forming a new doorway that hadn't been there before. Josh hesitated momentarily, but then he knew he had to follow where the key was leading him. He stepped through the doorway and found himself in a completely different room, filled with even more mysterious objects and treasures.

JOSH COULDN'T BELIEVE his luck. He had stumbled upon something incredible and knew he had to explore every inch of this hidden world. He felt a sense of excitement coursing through his veins, and he knew this was just the beginning of his adventure.

AS HE MADE HIS WAY through the chamber, he noticed something odd in the corner of his eye. It was a small, ornate box hidden behind a pile of other artifacts. Josh felt a sudden impulse to open the box, reaching for it eagerly.

AS HE OPENED THE BOX, he was in disbelief. Inside the box was a small, intricately carved amulet glowing softly with an otherworldly light. Josh knew that this was no ordinary amulet. It was ancient and powerful, and he could feel the energy radiating off of it in waves.

WITHOUT THINKING, HE picked up the amulet and placed it around his neck. As soon as it touched his skin, he felt an energy coursing through his body. He closed his eyes and concentrated, trying to understand what was happening to him.

WHEN HE OPENED HIS eyes again, he saw that the room around him had changed. The walls were covered in strange, glowing symbols, and the air was thick with magic and power.

JOSH KNEW THAT HE HAD unlocked something incredible, and he knew that he had to explore this new world to its fullest. He set down a new corridor, feeling the amulet pulsing against his skin with every step.

AS HE WALKED, HE SAW something coming towards him. It looked like an animal from a distance, but as it got closer, he realized it was like nothing he had ever seen. It was a creature with the head of a lion and the body of a serpent, and it moved with deadly grace.

JOSH FELT HIS HEART racing as the creature slithered closer to him, its eyes fixed on him with a dangerous intensity. He knew that he had to act fast if he wanted to survive.

INSTINCTIVELY, HE RAISED his hand, and a sudden burst of energy shot out from his fingertips. The creature recoiled, hissing angrily, but Josh didn't back down. He concentrated, focusing all his power on his hand, then released it in a powerful blast.

THE CREATURE LET OUT a deafening roar as it was struck by the blast, and then it fell to the ground, dead. Josh stood over it, panting and sweating, but he felt a surge of triumph coursing through his veins. He had just defeated a creature, unlike anything he had ever seen. "What's going on, Josh wondered. "Now what," Josh thought, scanning the room for an escape.

AS JOSH LOOKED AROUND the room, he noticed that the symbols on the walls were beginning to glow brighter, and he could feel the energy in the room growing more intense. He knew that he had to find a way out and fast.

HE SAW A DOOR ON THE opposite side of the room and made a run for it with the amulet around his neck pulsing with power. As he got closer, he saw the door covered in strange symbols but didn't hesitate. He reached out and placed his hand on the door, and he could feel the amulet's power surging through him. Suddenly, the symbols on the door began to glow, and then the door opened, revealing a blinding light beyond.

JOSH SHIELDED HIS EYES and stepped through the doorway onto a comprehensive, flat platform. A square hole cut into each of the four walls led into pitch-black tunnels carved in soil, brick, and stone. Each tunnel was wide enough for one man to enter, but there was no way to tell which would lead to safety. Josh looked back at the door he had just come through. It was gone except for a few scraps of wood hanging in the frame. The door had closed behind him and disappeared. A Wall had replaced it. Josh could hear his name being called as he scanned the many tunnels ahead of him. "Josh," the voices called. They sounded familiar. As he walked further, he noticed human hands moving through what looked like jail cell bars. As he got closer, he shone his flashlight toward the arrows.

IT WAS SOME OF THE kids from camp. "What are you guys doing here?" Josh asked them. "They were looking for you," one of the kids blurted out. "Who was?" Josh asked. "The cult," another kid whispered, fear etched on his face. "They've been trying to find the amulet you have. They'll stop at nothing to get it."

JOSH FELT A SENSE OF panic rising in his chest. He knew that he was in grave danger. "They locked us in this cage until they find you," one of the kids yelled out, "Run, I don't think they are going to hurt us. They said you have taken their power from them," said one of the boys. Josh's heart raced at the mention of the cult. He had heard rumors about them before, but he never thought that they even existed.

WITH THE AMULET STILL pulsing against his chest, Josh knew he had to act fast to escape the cult's grasp. He looked around at the tunnels, deciding which one to take. Suddenly, he noticed a faint glow from one of the tunnels, and he knew it was his only chance.

HE RAN TOWARDS THE tunnel, his heart pounding in his chest. As he got closer, he could feel the energy in the amulet growing more robust, and he could hear the sounds of the cult members searching for him.

JOSH KNEW THAT HE HAD to keep moving, and he sprinted down the tunnel, his feet pounding against the hard ground. As he ran, he could feel the walls closing in around him, and he knew that he had to find a way out before it was too late.

SUDDENLY, HE SAW A faint light up ahead, and he knew that it was his only chance. He ran towards it. As he approached the light, he realized it was daylight filtering through a small opening in the tunnel wall. Josh pushed hard at the wall, and it gave way with a loud creaking sound. He climbed out into the open air, gasping for breath.

HE LOOKED AROUND, TRYING to get his bearings, and saw that he was in a dense forest. The sun was shining down on him, and he could hear the sounds of birds singing in the distance. Suddenly, he heard a twig snap behind him, and he spun around, ready for whatever was coming.

JOSH RECOGNIZED THE kids from camp he had just spoken to locked in the cage, and his face drained of color. "Josh, here you are," one of them shouted pleadingly. The other kids pressed forward, voices urgent. "Everyone has been looking for you - where have you been?" another yelled. Josh looked around, confusion washing over him. "What do you mean? I just saw all of you in a cage," he stammered, fear gripping his throat. "A cage?" you got to do better than that, " one of the boys replied as the group laughed. "You guys just spoke to me in the cave over there," Josh insisted. "You got a real imagination," one of the boys relied upon as the rest laughed.

JOSH COULDN'T BELIEVE what he was hearing. Had it all been in his head? Was the amulet messing with his perception of reality? He shook his head, trying to clear his thoughts, but the kids were still staring at him with confusion etched on their faces.

"NEVER MIND," JOSH MUTTERED, feeling defeated. "Let's just get back to camp." As they walked back, Josh couldn't help but think that something was off. He couldn't shake the feeling that the amulet was still pulsing with power, even though he had taken it off hours ago. He kept his hand tightly around his necklace, hoping it was all in his head.

WHEN THEY FINALLY ARRIVED back at camp, Josh felt relieved. He was ready to put the whole ordeal behind him and focus on having a good time with his friends. But as he walked into his cabin, he saw something that made his blood cold. There, on his bed, was the amulet.

EPILOGUE

Sometimes when we look into the dark, we see nothing. Other times we know what our minds want us to see. What Josh saw wasn't a figment of his imagination but real. But the amulet had taken hold of him, and even as he tried to forget the experience, it would not be forgotten.

SHADOW OF THE BEAST

I never knew grade six could be hard until I lived through it. I was never a school fan, and most people thought I had a learning disability until I proved them wrong.

BUT IT WASN'T JUST the academics that made grade six unbearable. It was the social dynamics. I was never one to fit in, and that made me an easy target for bullies. They would taunt me on the playground, call me names in class, and even vandalize my locker. I tried my best to ignore them, but it was tough.

ONE DAY, AFTER A PARTICULARLY grueling day at school, I took a shortcut home through the woods. It was a path that few people knew about. Walking deeper into the woods, I heard a rustling in the bushes. Wild animals were known to live in this part of the forest, and I hoped it wasn't one of them coming out to hunt me down. But then I saw what looked like a beast.

IT WAS MASSIVE, WITH shaggy fur and sharp, pointed teeth. It growled at me, and my fear turned to panic as I realized it was getting closer. I stumbled back, my heart racing, my mind filled with terror. My thoughts raced as I tried to figure out what to do. Should I run? Should I stay still?

BUT THEN SOMETHING strange happened. The beast stopped growling, and instead, it started to pant. It looked up at me with its bright, intelligent eyes, and I realized it wasn't just a wild animal. It was a werewolf.

I HAD ALWAYS BEEN FASCINATED by legends of werewolves, but I never thought they were real. Yet here was one before me, and it seemed to be trying to communicate with me. With a start, I realized that it was trying to tell me something. It was telling me to escape, or I would die.

AS I TURNED TO RUN, the werewolf followed me. My heart raced as I tried to keep pace, but the beast was too fast. It easily kept up with me, and I knew it was only a matter of time before it caught me.

BUT THEN THE WEREWOLF surprised me again. It stopped and turned to face me. It growled, baring its teeth, and I thought it would attack me. But instead, it lowered its head and sniffed at me.

I STOOD FROZEN, UNSURE of what to do. The werewolf's hot breath washed over me, and I felt its powerful muscles tense. But then it stood up and backed away from me. It tilted its head as if it was studying me, and then it turned and disappeared back into the woods.

I STOOD THERE, HEART racing, trying to understand what had happened. Had I really just encountered a werewolf? And why had it let me go? I ran home to tell my best friend Jake, who I knew wouldn't believe me.

BUT I HAD TO TELL SOMEONE. I burst through the front door of my house, out of breath and still trembling from the encounter with the werewolf. I found my friend Jake in the kitchen, munching on a bag of chips and watching TV.

"JAKE, YOU WON'T BELIEVE what just happened to me," I said, panting. "I saw a werewolf in the woods." Jake's eyes widened in disbelief. "A what? You must be joking."

"I'M NOT JOKING, I SWEAR. It was huge, with shaggy fur and sharp teeth. And it was trying to communicate with me. "Jake took a long look at me, then said, "Okay, let's go check it out. I want to see this werewolf for myself."

I HESITATED, UNSURE if I wanted to return to the woods where the werewolf lurked. But Jake was insistent, so I reluctantly followed him back into the forest.

AS WE WALKED DEEPER into the woods, it became pitch dark. It was hard to see. I knew Jake was scared. We walked silently, the only sounds being our footsteps crunching on the fallen leaves and twigs. I could tell that Jake regretted his decision to come with me. But I had to show him that I wasn't lying and saw a werewolf.

SUDDENLY, WE HEARD a low growling in the distance. My heart leaped into my throat, and I knew the werewolf was nearby. Jake and I froze, and I could feel his body tense beside mine.

THEN, OUT OF THE DARKNESS, the werewolf appeared. It was even bigger and more imposing in the dim light of the forest. Its fur was matted and dirty, and its eyes glinted in the dark.

JAKE'S SCREAM PIERCED the night as the werewolf lunged towards us, its eyes blazing with primal rage and its saliva dripping from razor-sharp fangs. Panic engulfed me as I realized we had no chance against this monster until it paused mid-attack and did something nobody could have anticipated.

THE WEREWOLF SPOKE. Its deep, gravelly voice echoed through the silent forest. "Stop! I mean you no harm," it said, its eyes locked onto mine. "I could have killed you before, but I didn't. I let you go. And now you come back here with a friend?"

JAKE AND I STOOD THERE, frozen in shock. A werewolf that could talk? It was beyond anything we could have ever imagined.

"Why did you let me go?" I asked, my voice shaking.

THE WEREWOLF LET OUT a low growl as if recalling a painful memory. "I was cursed many years ago. I didn't ask for this life, but now I'm stuck with it. I can't control my transformation, and I'm constantly afraid of hurting someone." A deep sadness in the werewolf's eyes filled me with empathy. It was like looking into the eyes of a wounded animal.

"BUT THAT DOESN'T MEAN you have to hurt innocent people," I said, trying to reason with the beast. "There has to be another way."

The werewolf let out a bitter laugh. "You think I haven't tried? I've tried every remedy, every potion, every magic spell. But when the full moon rises, I lose all control. It's like a switch is flipped, and I become a monster." Jake and I exchanged a worried glance. Clearly, the werewolf was in pain, and we didn't know how to help.

THE WEREWOLF TILTED its head to the moonlight and unleashed a chilling, guttural howl that seemed to shake the earth beneath us. A thunderous chorus of other wild beasts answered its call from deep in the woods, an eerie reminder of its power over them. "I must go now," it growled with a brilliant smile. "But if you tell anyone about what you have seen tonight...if you whisper my secret...I will hunt you down like a dog."

WITH THAT, THE WEREWOLF disappeared into the darkness, leaving Jake and me alone in the woods, shaken and unsure of what to do next. We exchanged a glance, still in shock from the encounter, and then began to return to town.

AS WE WALKED, I COULDN'T shake the image of the werewolf's sad, intelligent eyes from my mind. I knew it was in pain and didn't want to hurt anyone. But I also knew it was dangerous, and we couldn't ignore its existence. Jake and I agreed to keep the encounter a secret, not wanting to risk the werewolf's wrath. But I also knew that we had to do something. We couldn't just let the curse continue to control the werewolf's life.

DESPERATELY SEARCHING for answers, I began a frenzied investigation into the secrets of werewolves and their dreaded curses. For weeks, I inhaled books, interrogated experts, and scoured cyberspace to find any information to help me break free.

AFTER SEARCHING FOR hours, I finally found a hidden entrance to a cave. After I had slipped inside, the air was noticeably still and quiet compared to the forest. The only sound was that of water dripping from the rock above me. The ground was slick from mud and moss, but there were places where it had been worn down by foot traffic, leading off deeper into the cave. A place like this would be a pilgrimage site for those seeking wisdom.

AT LAST, I CAME ACROSS an ancient-looking book with a cryptic passage that held my sought answer.

It was filled with ancient symbols and incantations and seemed to be written in a language that was no longer spoken. But I could sense that it held the key to breaking the curse that had befallen the werewolf.

I KNEW IT WAS A LONG shot, but I had to try. I returned to the woods, alone this time, and called out to the werewolf. It took a few minutes, but eventually it appeared. It was bigger than I remembered, and its eyes held a mixture of fear and curiosity.

"WHAT DO YOU WANT?" it growled, eyeing me warily.

"I think I can help you," I said, holding up the ancient book. "I found this, and it might have a way to break the curse that made you a werewolf."

THE WEREWOLF'S EYES flashed with shock as it leaped towards me, its claws extended and teeth bared. "How did you get that?! That's an ancient book of powerful magic, hidden for centuries, yet here you have it!" Its voice dripped with disbelief and barely suppressed rage.

BUT I STOOD MY GROUND, holding the book tightly in my grasp. "I found it in a cave. It holds the key to breaking the curse that plagues you." The werewolf hesitated, its eyes flickering between me and the book. I could see the war brewing behind its eyes, the struggle between its fear and desire for freedom.

FINALLY, IT LET OUT a low growl and took a step back. "Very well. Show me what you have found." I opened the book and began to recite the incantation, my voice shaking with nervousness. The werewolf watched me intently, its eyes shining with hope.

AS I SPOKE THE LAST word, the book seemed to come alive, its pages glowing with an otherworldly light. The werewolf let out a howl that shook the ground beneath us, and I knew the curse had been broken.

FOR A MOMENT, THE WEREWOLF stood there, stunned by the sudden change that had come over it. Then, slowly and hesitantly, it began to transform. Its fur receded, its claws retracted, and its eyes lost feral glint. When the transformation was complete, what stood before me was no longer a monster but a human being.

THE MAN STUMBLED FORWARD, disoriented by the sudden rush of sensations that came with his newfound humanity. Tears streamed down his face as he gazed up at me in gratitude.

"THANK YOU," HE WHISPERED, his voice choked with emotion. "I never thought I would be free from that curse. I never thought I could live a normal life again."

I PLACED A HAND ON his shoulder, feeling the warmth of his skin under my fingertips. "It was nothing," I said, trying to downplay the enormity of what had just happened. "I'm just glad I could help."

THE MAN LOOKED UP AT me, his eyes filled with a newfound sense of hope and wonder. "You have given me a second chance," he said, his voice trembling with emotion. "I will never forget what you have done for me."

AND JUST LIKE THAT, the encounter that had started with fear and uncertainty had ended with a sense of hope and possibility. The man thanked me repeatedly before disappearing into the woods, a free and happy human being once more.

AS I WALKED BACK TO town, my mind whirled with the possibilities of what I had just witnessed. It was a moment that would stay with me for the rest of my life, a reminder of the transformative power of magic and the resilience of the human spirit.

AND AS I LOOKED UP at the moon that had once been a beacon of death and despair, I couldn't help but feel a sense of wonder and awe. In its light shined a truth that connected us all. For in that moment, I knew that anything was possible.

THE TOWN THAT DISAPPEARED

Kyle walked into the hallways of Danton High School, feeling an aura of mystery and unease. He had moved to the small midwestern town only two weeks ago, and already he sensed something strange about the place. Everyone was silent and unnaturally solemn as if they were living in a dream. He glanced around in confusion at the other students, who seemed much older than him.

HIS MOTHER HAD INSISTED on moving here, and he had reluctantly complied. It was a town of only three thousand people, and the school only had around two hundred students and fifteen teachers, so the atmosphere was always quite somber. The buildings were old and decaying, but there was something comforting about them, something that made him feel as if he belonged there.

HE TRIED TO FOCUS ON his classes, but he couldn't ignore the sense of mystery that seemed to hang in the air. No one seemed to talk about their families or where they came from, and the adults appeared to be far too old for the roles they held.

Still, he was determined to uncover the secrets of Danton High and the town itself. He was sure there had to be a reason why everyone seemed so old and so quiet, and he was determined to find out what it was. He was convinced that he would find the answer if he searched hard enough.

JUST THEN, HE HEARD someone calling his name. He turned to see a girl with long brown hair and bright blue eyes. She smiled at him, and he felt his heart skip a beat.

"Hi, I'm Gwen," she said. "I'm in your English class."

"Oh, uh, nice to meet you," he replied, feeling his cheeks flush slightly.

GWEN SMILED AGAIN AND then gestured to a nearby wall. "You know, this school is pretty creepy. I know the others can't tell, but I can feel it in the air. It's like something's wrong here, you know?"

HE NODDED, FINDING himself strangely drawn to her. He wanted to ask her more questions, but it felt too awkward. He just nodded again.

"ANYWAY, IT'S NICE TO meet you," she said before walking away.

He watched her go, feeling a strange mixture of apprehension and excitement. She was right; something was wrong in Danton. He just didn't know what yet.

AS KYLE WALKED THROUGH the halls, his gaze lingered on the people around him. They all seemed so old and tired, like they had endured things that no one should ever bear. He couldn't shake the feeling that something was off about this place. The more he thought about it, the more he realized that the people weren't the only thing that felt off. The whole town seemed stuck in time; it was as if they were all living in some kind of time loop.

HE CONTINUED EXPLORING the town, trying to piece together the puzzle of Danton. It wasn't until he stumbled upon a hidden corner of the town that he finally found a clue.

He had been walking down a deserted alleyway when he saw her. She was a beautiful woman with long flowing hair and piercing green eyes. She was standing in front of a door that said, "Do Not Enter Unless Authorized By The Mayor.

"EXCUSE ME," KYLE SAID, approaching her. "What's behind that door?"

The woman looked at him, her eyes cold and calculating. "That's none of your concern," she said dismissively before turning and walking away.

KYLE WAS INTRIGUED. He knew that there was something important behind that door, and he was determined to find out what it was.

HE WAITED UNTIL THE woman was out of sight before approaching the door. He reached for the handle, but it wouldn't budge. It was locked. As he turned around, there was a man hunched over. He had to be over ninety years old, with wrinkles dominating his face.

"CAN I HELP YOU, SON?" the old man asked, his voice surprisingly strong. Kyle felt a shiver run down his spine as he looked into the old man's eyes. There was something dangerous there, something that made Kyle feel like he was in over his head.

"Uh, I was just curious about what's behind that door," he said, gesturing to the locked entrance.

THE OLD MAN'S EYES narrowed. "That's none of your concern, boy," he growled. "Now go on, get out of here before I call the authorities." Kyle didn't move. He was too curious, too intent on finding out what was behind that door. He had a feeling that it was something important, something that could explain the strange occurrences in Danton.

"PLEASE," HE SAID, HIS voice barely above a whisper. "I just need to know. I won't tell anyone." The old man looked at him for a long moment, his expression unreadable. Finally, he sighed and shook his head. "You're not going to give up, are you?" he asked.

KYLE SHOOK HIS HEAD, his heart racing with excitement and fear.

The old man sighed again and pulled a key from his pocket. "Fine," he said. "But you have to promise me that you won't tell anyone what you see inside."

Kyle nodded eagerly, feeling like he was on the cusp of a major discovery. The old man unlocked the door and then gestured for Kyle to enter.

As Kyle stepped inside, he was hit with the smell of must and decay. The room was dimly lit, with only a few flickering bulbs overhead. In the center of the room was a large, old-fashioned machine with levers and dials and buttons.

"WHAT IS THIS?" KYLE asked, his eyes wide with amazement.

The old man approached him, his face serious. "This is the time machine," the old man said gravely. "It's what keeps the people of Danton young and the town stuck in time. It was invented by the founder of

Danton, who wanted to create a utopia where people could live forever without aging or dying."

KYLE FELT HIS JAW DROP in disbelief. He had always thought that time travel was just a fantasy, but here it was, right in front of him. He couldn't even begin to imagine the power and knowledge that came with controlling time.

"BUT WHY KEEP IT A SECRET? Why not share it with the world?" Kyle asked, feeling a sense of urgency in his voice.

The old man shook his head sadly. "After the founder passed away, the town council took control of the machine. They didn't want anyone else to know about it, fearing that the outside world would try to take it away from them. They keep the machine running, but it's only a matter of time before it fails. The council has been keeping it a secret for so long that no one knows how to repair it."

Kyle felt a sinking feeling in his chest. He had always dreamed of discovering something amazing, but he had never considered the consequences of his actions. "What happens when it does fail?" he asked, his voice barely above a whisper.

The old man's eyes were filled with sadness. "The people of Danton will start to age and die like normal. The town will crumble and fall apart. It will be the end of everything we've worked for."

KYLE FELT A SENSE OF responsibility wash over him. He had stumbled upon a secret that could change the course of history, but he now realized that it was not his place to reveal it to the world. The people of Danton had made their decision, and he had to respect it.

"I WON'T TELL ANYONE," he said, looking the old man in the eyes. "I promise." The old man nodded, and Kyle felt a weight lifted off his shoulders. He turned to leave but then hesitated.

"Is there anything I can do to help? To keep the time machine running?" he asked, feeling a sense of obligation to the people of Danton.

THE OLD MAN SMILED at him, a glint of hope in his eyes. "Yes," he said. "There is one thing you can do. The machine requires a special mineral to function, which can only be found in a specific cave outside of town. We've been running low on it for months now, and we don't have anyone who can go retrieve it."

Kyle felt a surge of excitement. "I'll do it," he said without hesitation. The old man looked at Kyle. "Once you come to this town, you can't leave. Don't you understand this town only exists back in time?"

KYLE'S HEART SANK. He had been so caught up in the excitement of finding the time machine that he hadn't thought about the consequences. The fact that he was stuck in Danton, unable to leave, was a reality he hadn't considered.

"BUT I HAVE A LIFE OUTSIDE of this town," Kyle protested weakly.

The old man shook his head. "Once you're here, you're here for good," he said firmly. "But if you retrieve the mineral and bring it back, we'll make sure you're taken care of."

KYLE WEIGHED HIS OPTIONS. On the one hand, he could stay in Danton forever and help keep the town alive. On the other hand, he could leave and never look back but risk the people of Danton suffering the consequences of the time machine's failure.

He took a deep breath and made his decision. "I'll do it," he said, his voice solid and resolute.

THE OLD MAN NODDED. "You could die if you leave or not find your way back," proclaimed the old man. Kyle's heart raced with fear. He had always been an adrenaline junkie, but risking his life for a mineral was something he had never done before.

"But I have to do it," he said, his voice firm. "The people of Danton are counting on me."

THE OLD MAN SIGHED but nodded in agreement. He handed Kyle a map and a flashlight. "The cave is about a mile outside of town," he said. "The mineral is in a chamber at the back of the cave. Be careful, and come back to us safely."

KYLE NODDED, FEELING a sense of determination wash over him. He would do whatever it took to keep the people of Danton alive. He turned and headed out the door, taking his first steps on a journey that would change his life forever.

AS HE WALKED TOWARDS the cave, he couldn't help but feel a sense of foreboding. He had never been afraid of anything before, but now he was. He mainly worried about saving Gwen even though he had just met her.

KYLE PUSHED HIS WORRIES aside and focused on the task at hand. He had to retrieve the mineral and bring it back to Danton before it was too late. As he made his way through the forest towards the cave, he couldn't shake the feeling that he was being watched. He heard the rustling of leaves and the snap of branches, but when he turned around, there was no one there.

He quickened his pace, the flashlight beam bouncing along the rough terrain. The cave entrance loomed ahead of him, dark and foreboding. He took a deep breath and stepped inside, the musty smell of damp earth and rock filling his nostrils.

HE HEARD A FAINT WHISPERING sound as he made his way deeper into the cave. It sounded like a voice, but he couldn't make out what it was saying. He tried to ignore it and focused on finding the mineral.

AFTER WHAT SEEMED LIKE hours, he finally reached the chamber where the mineral was supposed to be. But as he approached, he saw that something was wrong. The mineral was missing, and in its place was a note. Kyle's heart sank as he read the note. It was a threat from someone who knew about the time machine and wanted to use it for their own purposes.

"BRING ME THE TIME MACHINE, or I'll make sure the people of Danton suffer," the note read. Kyle knew he had to act fast. He grabbed the note and ran out of the cave, back towards Danton. He couldn't let anyone use the time machine for evil purposes.

As he approached Danton, he saw that the town was in chaos. People were screaming and running in every direction. Kyle quickly realized that the time machine had failed and the people of Danton were aging rapidly.

KYLE SPRINTED TOWARDS the town center, his heart pounding wildly. When he arrived, he saw a white wall of fog surrounding the main buildings, eating away at them until they were nothing more than wispy particles in the air. "No!" Kyle shouted as he watched helplessly. He could almost feel time melting away from him, like sand through an hourglass. In the distance,

the sight of Gwen waving her arms and yelling was enough to send chills down Kyle's spine. His fingers clenched into fists as he started pushing his way through the throngs of people, his heart thudding in his chest like a bass drum. With every step he took toward her, Kyle felt as if he were walking deeper into the jaws of hell, but he knew that he couldn't leave Gwen alone.

HE HAD TO REACH HER before it was too late. "Follow me!" Gwen yelled. Kyle started to follow until he realized that they were heading toward the time machine. He couldn't let anyone use it for evil purposes.

"GWEN, WE CAN'T GO THERE!" Kyle shouted, trying to grab her arm. But Gwen shook him off. "We have to try!" she yelled back. "We have to do something!" At that moment, Kyle realized that Gwen was aging quickly by the second.

HER ONCE YOUTHFUL FEATURES were rapidly deteriorating, and her voice was becoming weaker and strained. Kyle could feel his own body starting to weaken as well, but he pushed through the pain and ran after her.

WHEN THEY REACHED THE time machine, they saw a figure standing in front of it, a dark shadowy figure with glowing red eyes.

"I've been waiting for you," the figure said, its voice cold and menacing. "Give me the time machine, and I'll spare your lives."

Kyle and Gwen exchanged a look, and then they both charged toward the figure. They knew they couldn't let him have the time machine, not after all the chaos it had caused.

THE FIGURE WAS SURPRISINGLY agile, dodging their attacks with ease. But Kyle and Gwen were determined, and they kept up their assault. Finally, the figure stumbled and fell, and Kyle delivered the final blow.

GASPING FOR BREATH, Kyle looked up and saw that the fog had dissipated. The town was still standing, and the people who had been running around in panic were now standing in stunned silence. Kyle and Gwen had saved the day.

AS THEY CAUGHT THEIR breath, the old man from the shop stepped forward, his eyes filled with awe and gratitude. "You did it," he said, clapping Kyle on the back. "You saved us all."

Kyle grinned, feeling a sense of accomplishment wash over him. He had never felt so alive.

BUT AS HE LOOKED AROUND at the people of Danton, he realized that he still couldn't leave. He was stuck in this town forever.

Gwen must have sensed his disappointment because she took his hand and squeezed it. "We'll figure something out," she said, her eyes full of determination. "We'll make a life here together."

As Kyle heard an explosive roar, he whirled around in shock. The entire town had vanished, along with Gwen, as if it had never existed. Panic and disbelief tore through him like wildfire. In the distance, he could see his mother standing alone.

Kyle trudged forward, feeling the burden of loneliness weighing down upon him. The area around him was a barren wasteland that stretched on forever with no sign of life in sight.

EVERY STEP SAW HIS mother vanish a little more as if she were being pulled away from him by an unseen force. Desperately he ran forward, yet still, his mother faded until all that remained was the distant echo of her voice in his head.

KYLE'S FOOTSTEPS FALTER, his eyes fixated on the empty space where his mother had just stood. Her disembodied voice echoes in his ears, a sweet melody that turns sour as her words sink in. "I love you, son," she says, and Kyle feels like he's about to collapse. The world around him blurs into a hazy fog, and his arms and hands begin to fade away before his very eyes, leaving him feeling weightless and unanchored. With a sharp intake of breath, Kyle faces the horror of his own vanishing existence and struggles to cling onto whatever is left of himself.

KYLE SUDDENLY UNDERSTOOD that the town of Danton was not a place for the living but a gateway into the afterlife. His breath quickened, and his mind spun wildly as he felt himself being pulled into the murky abyss, leaving his physical form behind in a whirlwind of terror and dread.

FOR WHAT FELT LIKE an eternity, Kyle floated in the darkness. Time had no meaning in this place, and he had no sense of his own body. All he could feel was a sense of peace, a calmness he had never experienced.

EPILOGUE

Beyond the reaches of human imagination lays a town where our deepest fears take physical form. It's a place where souls are judged before their final resting spot, as familiar as life itself, yet infinitely colder and unforgiving. Kyle knows his fate has been sealed; he's trapped in this icy grip, frozen in a place that's both hauntingly beautiful and utterly terrifying. Death!

About the Author

Mortaza Torkhy is an eleven-year-old with a love for the supernateral, para-normal and horror.

Read more at https://www.thelackingcity.com/.

TRUE AMERICAN PUBLISHING

About the Publisher

As a boutique book publisher, we take on only a few new authors per year. We focus on building an author's brand, thereby directing more resources towards their overall success. Authors accepted by True American Publishing become creative partners, therefore, participating in their own success.

CPSIA information can be obtained
at www.ICGtesting.com
Printed in the USA
JSHW081134160723
44761JS00002B/74